Creek Street

Story by Janeen Brian

Illustrations by Alfredo Belli

Contents

Chapter 1

A Startling Happening

Jackson stared at the two large gaping holes that had been dug into the red clay riverbank and shook his head.

"Doorways?" he muttered. "People couldn't have lived in there." He couldn't believe it. He picked his way across the uneven ground and grasped one of the metal grilles that had been set in the doorway to prevent entry.

"Help! I'm a prisoner," Jackson joked to his parents and younger sister, Ivy, behind him.

"Yay!" she shouted. "Don't let him out." Running up to him, she cried, "What can you see in there? Are there any ghosts?"

"Yes," said Jackson.

Ivy halted, eyes wide. "There are not."

"No?" Jackson said in a taunting tone. "Come and see for yourself, little one."

Ivy spun around. *"Mum?"*

"No ghosts, Ivy," said their mum. She opened a tourism brochure. "But it says here that over a hundred and fifty years ago, about two thousand people dug homes all along this deep riverbank. Mostly miners and their families. They came to Australia to work in the copper mines here."

"That's silly," said Ivy. "They should've built houses."

Jackson peered closer. "They're like big rabbit holes. Wouldn't people suffocate?"

"I wouldn't want to live in there," said Ivy. "It smells dirty."

"Maybe families back then didn't have a choice," said their dad.

Jackson moved a few metres across to the other doorway and peered through the bars. It was the same as the one next door. Another dim, gloomy hole with an earthen floor and a blocked up window. His mum read more information out loud from the brochure, but Jackson stood gazing inside.

Something was not right.

On the back wall, shadows began to play and flicker. Jackson leant one way and then the other. It wasn't his shadow. The day was calm with a few light clouds, and hardly any sun could reach inside.

With a frown, Jackson eased himself closer, until his nose almost touched the bars. He was still struggling to fathom what the strange shadows were on the wall, when a sound reached his ears. No. It wasn't one sound, it was a tumble of sounds. But they were so faint, they could've drifted in from dreams.

Jackson stood rooted to the spot, but he took a tentative glance over his shoulder. Everything looked the same. His parents were chatting to Ivy, who was pleading for an ice cream.

"Maybe later, Ivy," their dad said.

Ivy's reply faded into silence. Above the dugouts, a couple of other tourists were walking towards the slope that led to the riverbank. But from what Jackson could make out, none of them were talking.

Yet, Jackson could hear something. Not specific words, just murmurings.

Shivers ran up and down Jackson's back, and his skin tightened with goosebumps. He suddenly felt as if he should've worn something warmer than a t-shirt.

And then, without warning, a rush of smells came on so strongly that Jackson could almost taste them. He quickly covered his nose.

What was going on?

In front of him was a doorway that led into a cave-like room. Around him grew tufted green grass, maybe where water once ran. Leaves fell from trees. Birds flew overhead. And yet … Jackson grasped the doorway bars and stared inside. There were shadows. And sounds. And smells.

But was it all *really* happening? How could it be?

"Jackson, you coming?" called his mum.

With a jolt, Jackson cried, "Yeah, I am! I'll meet you back at the car."

"Okay, we'll wait on the main street."

Jackson took a breath, slid his hand into his jeans pocket and drew out his phone. Holding it up between the bars, he selected the camera icon.

And clicked.

The bright light on the screen was the last thing Jackson saw before a swirl of air whirled him through a spiral of darkness. Round and round he went, as if he were a feather in the breeze. He was floating and flying, but his eyes were open, fearless.

Chapter 2

Back to Creek Street

Sometime later, maybe a second, or a minute, a shudder rippled through him as if he'd been turned inside out. He ran his fingers through his curly hair. Then, he slurped the last of his porridge, stood and straightened his suspenders over his shoulders.

Jack looked around. Everything was as usual.

Shadows from the kitchen lantern danced across the walls. The air smelled of damp clothes drying, wood burning and something bubbling in a pot on the stove.

From down the chimney flue came a voice, yelling, "Butcher here, missus! Was you wanting meat for a nice stew?"

"Yes!" Jack's mam shouted back up the chimney. "I'll send my son up with the money." To Jack, she said, "Get a coin from the burglar safe.

I have to feed baby Clara. She's starting to fret." His mother hurried into the other room of their dugout with Clara in her arms.

Jack took a knife and set a stool near the stove. He had to scrape out a section of whitewashed wall before he could reach into the cavity. He pulled out a small cloth bag, took out a coin and slid the bag back into the hole. Later, his mam would cover the hole over and smear the earth with whitewash. Then, it would look like the rest of the wall. Their savings would be burglar-safe again.

"Take a dish," his mam called.

Jack gave the wooden door a firm nudge with his shoulder. He stepped outside and sucked in a sharp breath. The chill wind swept in from the low hills, past the copper mines and across the wide river, and bit his cheeks and ears. He wished he'd worn his jacket. By the time he'd climbed the rough steps to the top of the riverbank, he was puffing, but he was still cold.

"Mornin'," said the butcher. Wearing a dirty apron, a round-faced man stood next to an empty flour barrel. It was set there as a chimney pot for the stove in the dugout below. On the barrel was a board and a slab of meat. With a flourish that impressed Jack, the butcher drew a large knife from his belt and sliced off a fresh piece of meat before slapping it on Jack's dish.

Jack handed the butcher a coin.

"Thank 'ee," said the butcher with a nod.

Once back inside, Jack put the dish with the meat on a small shelf. It was one of many shelves his father had dug into the walls in the main room. His mother's best plate had a special shelf of its own. The clock sat on another. And that clock was ticking closer to school time.

Jack grabbed his jacket and began buttoning it over his suspenders and shirt. His little brother,

Thomas, was stacking small logs and knocking them down again.

"Bye, Thomas," said Jack.

Thomas grinned cheekily and grabbed on to Jack's leg.

"Let go, Thomas!"

But even as Jack dragged his leg, Thomas clung on, laughing.

"I have to go, you silly koala." Jack leant down and began to tickle his brother until the little boy wriggled and giggled and let go. "I'll see you soon," he said. "Before Da gets home from the mines. Bye, Mam!"

"Bye. Mind you shut that door good and proper. That wind would shave the hair off a pig."

Outside, Jack waved to Billy, his mate from three dugouts down. Billy was filling up the family's water barrel by the door.

"I still have to feed Honkers," Jack called to Billy. His words flew back at him in the wind, so he yelled louder. Billy held up his hand. He'd heard.

Honkers, the pig, snuffled in his pen, which had been built close to the dugout. Jack ladled slops into the pen, and Honkers slurped and snorted. "You're a greedy guts, Honkers!" laughed Jack, scratching the skin on the pig's back.

By now, the wind had stiffened. The next thing Jack knew, it whipped something long and white from his mother's washing line. Jack darted after it. He snatched it up seconds before it could land in the thin, mucky stream that trickled at the bottom of the river bed.

"Phew," he muttered. His face turned red as he pegged the garment back up. It was one of his mother's underskirts.

When Jack ran up to Billy, his mate smirked.

"I saw what you were pegging," he said with a teasing jab.

"So what?" Jack feigned a shrug, as if hanging up his mother's underwear was no big deal. "Come on," he said, quickly changing the subject, "or else old

Beaver Brain will set his friend on us."

The schoolteacher, Mr Blunt, walked with a limp and wore a tall black beaver hat. His *friend*, as he called it, was a whippy bit of cane that stung like billy-o.

The boys ran along the bumpy ground, calling out things they'd buy if they had a hundred pounds. A fortune!

Kids swarmed everywhere along Creek Street. Mothers called out greetings to each other, commented on the weather, emptied chamber pots and told their kids to keep back from the stream, "or your father will give you a what-for when he comes home from the mines."

Chickens clucked. Goats roamed. A few horses grazing nearby neighed.

"My name's Ben!" called a tame cockatoo. It was perched on a wheelbarrow outside the last dugout before the spot where the boys climbed up to cross to the school.

"We should train some animals and have a circus," said Billy. "We could train that cockatoo to say other things. That is, if old Grump-Face Dixon would let us borrow him. And I could teach my billy goat to jump through a hoop." Billy's eyes shone as he warmed to the idea.

"We could charge people to watch," said Jack.

"Then we'd really be rich," said Billy. "What about Honkers? What could he do? Sing? Tell jokes? Or dance around the maypole?"

Both boys burst out laughing.

Chapter 3

A Golden Disappearance

As they approached the Lucky Tree, Jack and Billy each stretched out a hand. Running past, they let their fingers brush across the smooth bark. The boys called it the Lucky Tree because it was one of the few large gum trees left in the area. Once, lots of trees had shaded the hills and valleys, but they'd been chopped down. The timber had been used to power machinery in the mines or to shore up the underground tunnels where the boys' fathers worked, hacking the rock for copper ore.

The schoolhouse was just beyond the tree. It was a small house, set back from a narrow, winding track.

"Are we late?" asked Jack, puzzled. "Where are the rest of the kids?"

The only sound was a crow calling mournfully above. The boys gulped as they exchanged glances.

"We *are* late, then," said Jack, crestfallen. It wasn't a good day when it started with a lashing

to the back of the legs. With his heart in his mouth, Jack trudged towards the front door.

"There's a note," he said.

All of a sudden, there came an explosion of noise. A mob of kids leapt out from around the side of the house, waving their arms, yelling and laughing.

"Ha! Ha!" cried Frank, the biggest kid of the lot. "Did we scare you?"

"No," chorused Jack and Billy, not letting on.

"He's gone," said Lizzie.

"Who? Beaver Brain?" asked Billy, open-mouthed.

"Dead?" asked Jack.

"No. He's left for the goldfields," Frank blurted out. "Went this morning. It's in the note."

"Isn't that a long way away?" asked Billy. "Must be hundreds of kilometres! He'll never make it with that limp."

"There are cartwheel tracks over there," said Lizzie, pointing. "And horse poo."

The kids all stared at each other. "No school," whispered Billy. His eyes danced.

For a long time, none of the kids moved. Then, a couple of kids began to fidget. A few giggled. The boys began to push each other, and soon they were all whooping and dancing wildly.

"I'm off," said Frank finally. "I'm going to climb that hill over there. Who wants to come?" A few other kids joined him. The rest wandered off in different directions, chattering about what they were going to do.

Billy glanced at Jack and raised his eyebrows, questioning.

Jack ran a hand through his dark, curly hair. "If I don't tell Mam what's happened, she'll be hopping mad when she finds out. Especially if I scarper off for the day. But if I do go home, I'll get chores."

"I know," said Billy, grim-faced. "Me, too."

Jack looked up to the blue skies and let out a long, noisy sigh.

Billy nodded, shoulders drooping.

"At least we didn't get the cane for being late," said Jack, hugging the Lucky Tree. "I wonder what we'll do every day if we don't go to school."

"I could start training my goat for the circus, and you could train Honkers."

The boys started walking. Jack kicked a clod of dirt along the way. "But what else?" he asked. "We mightn't get another teacher for ages."

"I dunno," said Billy. "Are you coming down here?"

"Yeah."

Jack followed his friend down the ladder alongside his dugout. "See ya, Billy. Good luck," he added with a grin.

"You, too."

Just after three o'clock, Jack's father trudged home from the mines. Jack took a basin of water, a sliver of soap and a rag outside so that his da could clean himself.

"That's better," his father said, once he was inside. He took a seat beside the stove and jigged Thomas up and down on his knee.

"Go faster!" cried Thomas.

"William," said Jack's mam, rocking Clara, "that schoolteacher, Blunt, he's no right to up and leave like that. Gold, indeed. What's wrong with copper?"

Da lifted Thomas off his knee and fetched a ball for him from a shelf. "I'm hearing more and more talk of it down in the mines, m'dear," he said. "John Pelligrew is thinking of heading to the goldfields. So are plenty of others. I can see it in their eyes."

Jack took a seat at the table to listen. What was going to happen to him?

"Still, m'dear, I agree," his father added. "It ain't right the way the teacher left." He turned to Jack. "I'll get you a job in the mines until another teacher is found."

Jack paled. But he knew better than to question his father's decisions.

"That's a good thing, son," said Jack's mother.

"You can sort through the copper ore in the pickey shed above the mines," said his father. "I'll speak to the person in charge tomorrow."

"You'll be a pickey boy," said his mother.

Jack nodded. At least he wasn't going underground. His thoughts flew to Billy. What were *his* parents planning to do with him?

Chapter 4

To the Pickey Shed

The next day, Jack discovered Billy had a job with the butcher.

"What will you be doing?" Jack asked.

"I don't know yet." Billy's mouth twisted in a wry grin. "I guess it will be something to do with meat!"

Jack laughed.

"But you'll only do it until we get another teacher," Jack said. "Right?"

"I suppose so," said Billy. But he looked no more certain than Jack was about how long he'd be a pickey boy. Or even about what a pickey boy did.

But his father only told him a little when Jack asked the following afternoon.

"You walk to the pickey shed and get there no later than seven o'clock. Be polite. Say you're my son. Then listen and learn."

"Yes, Da. Can't I walk with you?"

"No, son," said his father, patting Jack on the shoulder. "I leave even before the birds know it's a new day. You'll likely need a lantern as well. Take care in the dark."

Jack nodded. Ever since he was Thomas's age, he'd been warned about the dangers of falling into old mineshafts and large holes. There was a chance of getting hurt or disappearing out of sight if you fell in, with no one knowing where you were.

Jack didn't ask about money, even though being a pickey boy was a paid job. His wage would go straight to his mother to be put in the burglar safe. Perhaps, with a bit of luck, she might give him a coin now and then. If that happened, he could buy a marble or two from Mr Penglase's shop.

Imagine, both Billy and him working. And only a few days ago, they were sweating over the names of all the capital cities in the world. And reciting their times tables over and over, until Jack wanted to leap to his feet and shout, "I already know them inside out!"

Jack's bedroom was tiny. Earlier that year, he'd begged his father to dig out another room so that he didn't have to share with Thomas. Now, he had a small space for his bed and two shelves. One was for his clothes. The other was for his special things. On it was the encyclopedia he'd won as a school prize, his bag of marbles and a beautiful, shiny green stone.

Jack felt he'd only been asleep for a moment when his mother shook his shoulder and told him to get dressed.

"There's a bowl of porridge ready for you on the table. And a pasty for your lunch."

Jack yawned. His stomach was in knots, and he could barely swallow the porridge. He was lighting the lantern when Thomas wandered blearily up to him.

"Go back to bed," Jack whispered. Thomas clung to his brother as if he'd never see him again.

"Come along, Thomas," said their mother. "Say goodbye to Jack."

But Thomas let out a wail of distress, which then woke baby Clara. Their cries echoed around the clay walls of the dugout.

Jack pulled back the square of material that hung from the window. He was barely able to see through the darkness outside. He rubbed his arms and picked up the lantern and his lunch.

"Go, boy," said his mother. "Be good. Take care." And she gave him a peck on the cheek.

Jack started. His mam hardly ever kissed him.

"Bye, Mam," he said.

Dark clouds hung low across the valley in the distance. Jack yanked the door shut. Honkers gave a loud, startled grunt that almost shot Jack out of his breeches. After he'd caught his breath, he raised the lantern. Then, he carefully started to walk along the riverbank, close to the dugouts. The small, flickering flame meant he didn't trip over a miner's wheelbarrow or a wood heap. Or startle a nesting chicken. But the lantern's light didn't reach the creek, and he needed to find the footbridge to get across.

After a while, Jack noticed tiny lights dancing in the distance. It was a fine sight, and his breathing eased. He wasn't the only one, then, picking his way in the dark to the mines.

As he trudged along, the wind came at him in gusts. First from one direction, then the other. Jack hunched to keep from shivering, but the wind was sharper. It found gaps, sneaking into places where his jacket didn't meet and chilling the back of his neck and his ears below his cap.

Jack wished the darkness would ease and dawn would come. The spread of morning light would make walking much easier. He knew well enough that the drop to the creek was steep here, but trying to judge the whereabouts of the bridge was more difficult than he expected.

On any other day, he would've said, "Easy! I can find that bridge with my eyes closed."

From a distance came the *thump, thump, thump* of the mine machinery. That was the sound Jack needed to guide him to the mines. But his heart was thumping at twice that speed.

At last, he reached the wooden bridge. Despite not having a free hand to grip the rail, Jack managed to cross it without much trouble. Now, he only needed to scramble up the other bank of the river, and he'd be on level ground.

In the gloom, the tall chimneys and buildings of the mine rose like a town of its own. Jack had never been so close to it. He shuffled between buildings, around large mounds and past whims, which looked like large wooden barrels on poles. When they were turned by horses led by young boys, the whims could draw water up from the mines.

"Excuse me," Jack said to a man who'd just stepped out of a doorway. "Can you please tell me where the pickey shed is? I'm new."

The man extracted a clay pipe from his mouth. "You'll find it over there. Up them steps."

"Thank you," said Jack.

He soon saw he wasn't the first boy to arrive. He hoped he wasn't the last. At the top of the steps, a large man whose waistcoat strained against his belly was noting names in a book.

"Jack Treloar," said Jack. "I'm William Treloar's son."

"You look like him and all," said the man. "Right, I've got your name. Get yourself a seat at the bench. The boys will tell you what to do. Your father said you'll learn fast."

Jack felt a flutter in his stomach. He wasn't sure how much his father had said about him. He hoped he wouldn't disappoint.

Chapter 5

New Beginnings

In front of Jack was a long room with a wide table running down the middle. On either side were bench seats, and boys were scurrying to pick their favourite spot.

"Here, Charlie," came a cry.

"Over here, Stanley. Next to me."

"Quick, lift your feet, Albert."

Jack stood, overwhelmed, wondering where he should sit. Finally, he found a gap between two boys. They both turned to look at him.

"I'm Jack," he said.

"Harry," replied one.

"Arthur," said the other.

Jack stared at the empty table. "What do we have to do?"

"Wait."

Then, a mighty rumble came from somewhere, and ore began to tumble and clatter onto the table in a cloud of dust.

"Now, you pick," said Harry.

"What do I pick?"

"The rocks that got copper in it, this green-blue stuff, goes in that box. If it ain't got much, it goes in this one."

"And if it's got nothin' in it," said Arthur, "well, that's your lunch!" He roared at his own joke.

"You'd better get all that in your head pretty quickly," added Harry, "cos we get watched."

Jack picked up a piece of ore and turned it over and over, looking for telltale copper traces.

"Hey!" shouted a boy across the table. "You'll be out on your ear if you take your time like that."

Another kid called out, "Are you from Creek Street? Reckon I've seen you."

Jack put a rock in the second box and called back, "Yeah, I am."

"Me, too," came a chorus of voices.

Jack glanced about, looking for familiar faces.

"On with your work!" came the supervisor's loud command. "There's another load coming. And another after that."

"He always says that," said Harry.

"It's true, though," said Arthur with a sigh.

Jack was struggling to work at the same speed as the boys on either side of him when he heard the supervisor say to someone in the doorway, "You're late!"

Jack kept on working, pleased he'd at least made it to the pickey shed on time.

"I only just found out I was working here, sir," came the boy's response.

"Did you now? What's your name, then?"

"Billy. Billy Tregonning."

Jack leapt from his seat.

"Billy!" he gasped in delight. "Over here," he beckoned.

Billy gaped. A wide grin spread across his face.

"Hey, can you shove up?" Jack said to Harry and Arthur. "Billy's my mate."

Billy squeezed in and hissed, "What do I do?"

"I'll tell you, so that you can get going. Then you've got to tell me why you're here."

Jack felt weird explaining the job to Billy when he'd only been told himself a short while ago. "Got it?" he asked.

Billy nodded.

"Keep sorting, then," said Jack. "But what happened? You were supposed to be working for the butcher."

"I know. And I did. For one day. But then, when I went there this morning, there's no butcher."

"You don't mean –"

Billy nodded again. "He's gone as well. Off chasing the gold."

"Whoa!" Jack blew out a noisy breath. "So now there's no butcher?"

"There's a new man, but he didn't want me there. Told me to come here. Said there was always a place in the pickey shed, because kids get sick from the dust."

Jack pulled a face. Then he brightened. "But now we're together."

At break time, the boys strode out of the gloomy shed, eager to scramble down the steps and walk outside. They soon forgot about the cold and began to dart and dodge and chase each other in a game of tag. Others played leapfrog. Several kids squatted in the dirt, having drawn circles with sticks for a game of marbles. Jack looked on longingly.

"We'll bring our marbles tomorrow," he said to Billy.

"Yeah."

Together, they opened their cloth bags and shared their lunches. Above them, clouds shifted in the wind, but any gap was soon blotted out by the thick, dark smoke that belched continuously from the mines.

The rest of the day dragged. Jack had to shift often on the hard bench. He tried to ease his aching back and stretch his dirt-stained fingers so often, Harry whispered, "Can you stop your wriggling?"

"I'll try," said Jack, his eyes stinging from the dust.

To pass the hours, several of the boys chatted to each other in quiet tones. Others stifled laughter. Some kids who were feeling the cold draped hessian bags over their shoulders. It was the same kids who were constantly coughing and sniffing.

"When do we go home?" Jack whispered to Harry.

"When he rings the bell." Harry gestured towards the supervisor in his office.

"It's the best sound in the world," said Arthur.

Jack wiped his nose along the sleeve of his jacket. He could understand that.

"Least we don't get caned here," said Billy.

Chapter 6

Surprise Adventures

One day followed another, but Jack and Billy were pleased to be able to meet up every morning. And in the afternoons, they whooped and ran all the way home, glad of whatever sunlight there was.

"Our fathers don't get to see much sun, do they?" Jack said one day, as he tossed a stone into the air. "First, they work underground, and then when they come home, they're still underground."

"They have Sundays off," said Billy. "They can go outside then."

"Yes, I suppose," said Jack. "Unless they're in church. Or visiting. Or it's raining."

They were wandering along the side of one of the river's tributaries. There, the creek was narrower, and, in one part, it was only a muddy waterhole. Dugouts lined those banks as well.

"Hey, what's going on over there?" Jack stopped and pointed. "Look at those kids. What are they doing?"

Two strange boys were walking along the top of the riverbank dugouts and kicking over the flour barrel chimney pots.

Billy went to call out, but Jack pulled his arm. "Wait. What are they doing now?"

One of the boys suddenly dropped a line down a chimney. The other boy leant in, close as a shadow.

Jack and Billy watched, flabbergasted, as the first boy jiggled the line and then, moments later, jubilantly pulled it to the surface. There, hanging from the hook, was a piece of meat. It had been snatched out of a cooking pot on the stove below, and it was still steaming.

"Get him!" Jack cried. Together, he and Billy gave chase.

"Ha! Ha!" shouted the other boys. "Don't even try to catch us!"

"Get the one with the meat!" Jack shouted to Billy. "Forget about the other kid."

They chased him until they had him cornered. The boy tried to dodge them, but he nearly slipped off the edge of a dugout roof. His cap went flying.

"Not yours," said Jack, and he unhooked the meat.

Jack and Billy walked the boy down the bank and stood in front of the dugout the boys had stolen from. Billy knocked. A lady came to the door and stared at what was in Jack's hand.

"Here's your meat, missus, and here's a boy who wants to say sorry." Jack used his knuckles to prod the boy in the back.

"Sorry," he muttered.

The lady nodded and then turned to Jack and Billy. "I can't thank you enough," she said. "My husband's left me and our three children and gone off to the goldfields. That's all the meat we have."

"Do you need any wood chopped?" asked Billy.

"Oh!" The woman's eyes went wide with surprise. "That would be helpful."

"He'll do it," said Jack, and he pushed the boy forward. "Goodbye, missus," he added.

He and Billy waited nearby until the boy had begun chopping. Then they went off, nudging each other and grinning.

"Now what?" asked Billy.

"Let's go to the Lucky Tree," suggested Jack.

"Race you," said Billy.

They ran as fast as they could, reaching the Lucky Tree at almost the same time.

"It's a draw!" said Billy. But Jack forgot about the race when he saw what was on the ground. The wind had blown down several large dead branches, as well as a number of smaller ones.

"We could make a fort," Jack said, stooping to gather them together.

"Or," said Billy, "a raft!"

"Yeah!" said Jack with enthusiasm. "And float it down … where?"

"We could try the creek. There might be stretches up past the dugouts where it's deep enough."

Jack's eyes shone.

Once the boys had heaved the branches into a ragged pile, they stood, hands on hips.

"We need rope," said Jack, "to tie the branches together for the raft. Have you got any? I haven't."

"I'll ask Da. There might be some scraps at the mines. We could go look."

"Yeah, but right now, we need to hide these branches. If we drag them home, they'll end up as ash in the stove."

In the end, the best the boys could do was shove the branches into a hollow nearby. They then showered dry leaf litter and a couple of scraggy bushes over the top.

"Let's hope Frank and his mates don't find them first," said Jack, staring at their hidden treasure.

Chapter 7

Broken Dreams

The next day, the boys spent their break time searching for odd scraps of twine and parts of hessian bags – anything they could fashion into rope. It helped speed up the work day.

Jack was already wondering whether being in the pickey shed was better than a classroom after all. They mightn't be caned, but there was only one pathway after working in the pickey shed. That path was down – as a miner, underground. Jack wasn't sure about that path. But he didn't express his thoughts to anyone.

Billy still seemed keen on creating a circus.

"I don't reckon I'll get Honkers to do anything," Jack explained to Billy. "He grunts and snorts. That's it."

"What if you tried to get him to grunt or snort on command? With food," suggested Billy.

"I'll try," said Jack, although he thought training a goat to leap through a hoop might be easier.

"Let's go and speak to Grump-Face Dixon this afternoon. See if we can teach his cockatoo to say something funny."

After the bell rang, the boys ran all the way to Grump-Face Dixon's dugout.

"Yes?" said the old man, when the boys knocked on his door.

"Hello, Mr Dixon," said Billy. He'd put on a very posh voice, and Jack had to turn away before he laughed. "My friend here, Jack Treloar, and I have long admired your wonderful talking cockatoo. Now, we have come up with a marvellous idea of creating a circus, and we would love it if your cockatoo could be the star attraction."

By this time, Jack had his lips pressed tightly together. Mr Dixon's face was a picture. His frown was more crinkled than a dried creek bed. And he was glaring at Billy as if he was mad.

"Well, you can't," Mr Dixon said.

Not to be put off so easily, Billy continued. "We would be very careful with him, and we would acknowledge you, too, as his beloved owner and trainer. We might even extend your cockatoo's vocabulary."

Now Jack had to pretend he was having a coughing fit. He couldn't control his laughter any longer.

"Like I said earlier," Mr Dixon burst in, "and if your ears were as big as your mouth, you would've heard clear enough: you can't have Cockatoo. Not you. Nor anybody else. Because he's gorn."

No one spoke for a moment.

"Gorn?" queried Billy.

"Yes. Flown away. Gorn. Yesterday. And I'm still upset about it, so if you don't mind, take yourselves and your circus idea somewhere else!" He slammed the door shut.

Both boys stood in silence for a moment. Neither knew what to say.

"That's that, then," Billy said at last.

"I know where the bird's gone," said Jack.

"To the goldfields!" they both said together, and they ran away laughing until they were sore in the stomach.

Jack's father was leaning against the water barrel with a pipe in his mouth when Jack arrived home. His da's eyes were crinkled, and he was staring into the distance.

"Hello, Da," said Jack. He prodded the ground with a thin branch he'd carried from the Lucky Tree.

"Son!" His father removed his pipe and coughed. "I didn't see you coming."

"Do you need more water to clean up?"

"I reckon I'm shiny bright enough, thanks."

Jack smiled, but his father's voice sounded troubled. However, it wasn't up to him to ask his da anything further.

"Your mam's … a bit weepy," his father added in a quiet voice.

Jack opened the door. His mother was seated at the table, head down. Several strands of hair had come loose and were hanging down beside her face. She was rocking Clara. The baby grizzled and hiccuped as if she'd been crying for a long time.

Thomas sat in the corner, arms crossed, kicking at the edge of the mat.

"Hello, Mam," said Jack. He'd been keen to tell her the story of how he and Billy had caught a boy stealing food red-handed. But when his mam glanced up, the words dried up in his mouth.

"Hello, son," she said. Her voice was wavery, and her eyes were red.

It was then that Jack saw his mother's best plate on the table. The one she kept on a little shelf of its own. The one she treasured. The one she'd brought from Cornwall when they'd left to come to Australia. It was the only thing she had left that had belonged to her mother.

Now, it lay there in pieces. Broken.

Clara wailed.

"She's getting teeth," said his mam, looking away.

"How did the plate get broken?" asked Jack.

"It was an accident. Thomas wanted to help clean. He took the birch broom and waved it up high and … he didn't mean it."

Jack went across the room and picked Thomas up. The little boy put his head on Jack's shoulder. At that moment, the door opened and the wind rushed in, bringing with it all the noise from Creek Street. Jack's father stepped inside.

"Come now, William," said Jack's mother. "Jack will make you a nice cup of tea, and I'll get our dinner on."

"No, sit awhile."

Suddenly, there was quiet. Clara had fallen asleep.

"I will be needing to talk to you, m'dear."

"I'll set the baby down, William, and then you can be telling me what you have to say."

When his mother returned, Jack placed a cup of tea on the table and quietly put the bits of plate back on the shelf. He didn't know what else to do.

"You sit, too, Jack," said his father. "We're a family."

Jack sat on a chair he'd helped make from a packing case. Thomas climbed up on his lap.

"There's talk in the mines," Jack's father began. "Talk of the miners getting together and demanding more pay. Better pay for the work that's done."

"Getting together?" asked Jack's mam.

"Yes, m'dear. Against the owners of the mining company."

Jack's mother gasped. "But isn't that wrong?"

"What's wrong is that our wages are poor, so poor we can't afford to pay rent to get a house for our family. Meanwhile, the owners are getting fat on their backsides."

Jack's eyes opened wide at the rude word, but he kept his mouth shut.

"I'm just telling you. There's rumblings at this stage. But there's also rumblings of more miners, and others, leaving for the goldfields."

Jack straightened. So much talk about the goldfields.

"And, I have to say, m'dear, if there's gold for the picking –"

"William! You don't mean you'd go? And leave us? What would we do? We'd have no money, 'cept what we got saved. And what Jack brings in. How would we live?"

"We can discuss it all later, m'dear."

Jack's thoughts fled to the lady whose husband had left, who'd had her meat stolen. His heart lurched. He didn't want his father to go to the goldfields. But … but maybe Da meant for the whole family to go. To leave Creek Street forever.

Jack felt his body cave in on itself. This was his home. Billy was here. Soon, a new teacher would come, and they'd go back to school, and they would make a raft, and have adventures, and –

Thomas looked up at him and grinned. But the uneasiness Jack felt made it hard for him to smile back.

That night, he went to bed feeling as if the plate wasn't the only thing that was broken.

Chapter 8

Rain Brings Change

At first, Jack didn't hear the rain. There was no drumming sound in his bedroom. The thick earthen roof dulled the noise.

It was a different story, however, when he shuffled out for his breakfast. The gaps around the door and the window allowed the rain in, as well as the wind. The curtain glowed from occasional lightning flashes. It was going to be a rough, wet walk to the pickey shed. The only good thing about the morning was that it was a little brighter, which meant there was no need to carry a lantern. After turning up his collar, Jack pulled his cap down low and wedged his lunch, in its cotton bag, inside his jacket.

"Bye, Mam!" he called. "Bye, Thomas. Go back to bed now."

The morning light might have made Jack's way easier to see, but the rain was as solid as a curtain in front of him. The ground was muddy and slippery. And the creek was no longer a patchy stream. It was moving steadily, and it had even risen to the base of the footbridge.

By the time Jack reached the pickey shed, he was soaked, as were the other kids. Soon, the whole room smelled of damp clothes and boots. But not every kid was in their spot. There were a number of empty places.

"Those boys will have their pay cut," said Jack.

"Yeah," said Billy, wiping his face and pulling at a lock of Jack's hair. It hung wet and curly down the centre of his forehead. "Good weather for our raft, though."

"Can't wait," said Jack. At least Billy had gone off the idea of a circus.

But as the hours passed, the rain grew steadily stronger and louder. Boys inched away from the broken windows, complaining they were getting drenched.

"My mam will be cross," said Harry. "She left her washing outside."

"I forgot to cover up our chicken pen," said Arthur.

One boy looked outside and said in a serious voice, "That's rain, all right."

Jack and Billy exchanged glances. They weren't sure if the boy was joking or not.

"No break outside today, lads," said the supervisor. "But you can have some time off inside."

Jack and Billy both raised their eyebrows. But before they'd even had a chance to clamber out of their seats, a man rushed into the shed and spoke urgently to the supervisor. The supervisor grabbed the bell and rang it frantically.

"What?" cried a couple of boys in surprise. "We haven't even had a break!"

"Listen!" cried the supervisor in a grave tone. "Any kid from Creek Street, go home now! Get back to your families. The creek's up. There's a flood!"

There was a scramble to the door.

The rain was hard and heavy. It thudded on Jack's head.

Lightning flashed. Thunder rumbled. And Jack and Billy ran and ran, trying to keep each other from slipping and sliding. Jack was unable to imagine what Creek Street would look like. But before they reached the riverbank, they stopped. Frozen to the spot.

"The creek's gone," said Billy blankly. "It's a river now."

"No," said Jack, his voice shaking with fear. "It's a sea!" It was a monster of a sea, and the wind and rain were churning up waves. It had no boundaries, but rushed wherever it wanted.

And it was sweeping into the dugouts.

"No!" Jack screamed. And, as if the sound of his shout cleared his head, he saw. He really saw. It wasn't just water tearing its way downstream. Beds, barrels, goats, chickens, fences, chairs and other furniture were also being carried away. Jack raced closer. With his heart in his mouth, he scurried towards a rickety footbridge and scrambled across it as water lapped at the edges. Then, he tore towards his home. Water was swirling in the doorway of the dugout. Jack's mam was trying to scramble to safety, climbing up the riverbank while clutching Clara. Thomas was holding her other hand, but he kept slipping.

"Mam!" Jack screeched. "Mam!"

Thomas kept sliding down the bank, crying, and he was dragging their mam with him. Then he tumbled.

"Help!" Jack screamed into the chaos. "Someone, get my brother!"

A man jumped from a cart and skidded towards the riverbank. Thomas cried out.

As the water whooshed past him, a wooden box landed on the edge of the bank.

"Thomas!" shouted Jack's mother. "Grab the box!"

The boy turned towards her and, terrified, reached out and clasped the box.

The next minute, he and the box were swept away.

"Thomas!" Jack screamed. Billy had run to help his own family. Jack looked around, panic-stricken. He spotted a familiar tangle of eucalyptus branches just upstream. The branches from the Lucky Tree! They must have been washed out of the hollow.

Jack pulled the largest branch out of the tangle and raced down towards the narrowest part of the river, where it curved. "Thomas!" he called. "Here! I'm here!" He wedged his heels deep into the clay and held out the branch.

Thomas, pale and terrified, clung to the box. Both were being swept closer and closer to the spot where the river curved. Several people grabbed Jack around the waist to prevent him from toppling in. They were not a second too soon. The waters washed the box and Thomas towards the branch.

"Thomas!" Jack called. "Hang on, Thomas! Please hang on!"

And then … then …

What was that sound? A sudden noise, like the whine of a mosquito, was drilling into Jack's head. He was being called from a faraway place. Who was it? And why would someone cry out to him? Didn't they know he was needed here?

And then, just as swiftly as snuffing out a flame, all sound stopped. Jack was spinning and whirling in a dark mist, as if being swept into space.

What was happening? Was there somewhere else he should be? Could that be possible?

And then, amidst all the struggle, Jack knew. Somehow, he knew that this was not all there was. He had to leave this life, or he'd be trapped here forever.

"He's coming closer!" Sound rushed back as a woman shouted in his ear. "Can you get the branch out further?"

Jack's stomach churned. He knew he had to leave. But how could he? If he didn't act quickly, right now, his little brother might drown.

"Jack! Jack!" Thomas was howling.

Terror gripped Jack. If Thomas took even one hand off the box, he'd be gone. Lost to the raging waters.

“Nearly there, Thomas!” Jack cried. “Not much further. Hang on!”

Jack pushed the branch out. At the same time, he wrestled to keep it as close as possible to the surface. Any moment, he felt his arms would snap.

The box swerved closer. Closer. Closer. Thomas was choking, spluttering.

“Keep going, Thomas,” Jack yelled. “Hang on. Good boy. Hang on!”

The next minute, the box snagged against the branch. Jack's feet began to sink in the mud. What if he fell in, too? Frantically, he gripped the branch so hard his knuckles went white. The people behind him held on tightly. Then, using every scrap of energy he had, he pulled the branch against the force of the water and dragged the box and Thomas towards the edge.

As soon as Thomas was close enough, Jack cried in a hoarse voice, "Grab him! Please, someone grab him!" He flung the branch aside as tears trickled down his face. "Thomas," he sobbed. "You're safe now. You're safe."

That was all Jack could say. His mouth was empty of words, and his head was crowded with those other sounds that kept calling him. And, in a flash, he was spinning again. As he whirled in flickering darkness, parts of him shifted out of time and place.

He had to leave.

Chapter 9

Questions

Jackson ran.

He ran down the streets and along the footpaths, away from the dugouts. He ran and ran towards the town. He ran until he reached the main street. Then, he saw them.

His mum waved first. Ivy thrust her hands on her hips, pointing to the ice cream shop.

"You took *so* long," she said.

"Oh, Ivy," said Dad. "It was only fifteen minutes, if that. Did you enjoy looking at the dugouts, Jackson?"

Jackson stared at the cars as they zipped along the road. He stared at the people sipping coffee at the outdoor cafe. He stared at the families pushing prams and the kids swinging around a pole. He looked down at the clothes he was wearing: a t-shirt, jeans and sneakers. His holiday clothes.

Above him, the sun peeped through a few light clouds. He was warm and dry.

"What did you say, Dad?" he asked shakily.

"I asked if you enjoyed seeing the old ruins. They were washed out a long time ago."

"Yeah," Jackson mumbled. "I know. I was … it was …"

Tentatively, he reached inside his jeans pocket. His fingers gripped his mobile phone.

"Can we get ice cream *now*?" asked Ivy.

"Okay," said Dad, "but you're paying, Ivy." He laughed.

"Am not," said Ivy, with a grin. "Mum is. She said so. And she said she wanted two scoops with chocolate and mango. Didn't you, Mum?"

"I have to confess." Their mum held out her palms and nodded. "What flavour would you like, Jackson?"

Jackson didn't answer. He'd opened his phone and was gazing at a photo. A kind-faced lady in a long dress and an apron was standing beside a wood-burning stove. She held a baby in her arms. At her feet was a little boy. He was proudly pointing to a stack of logs. On the back wall was a faint shadow from a lantern.

And somewhere deep inside, Jackson knew who these people were and where they lived.

Still, questions filled his head to bursting. There was no room to think about what ice cream he'd like.

What became of Jack, the boy who lived with his family in Creek Street, who had a friend called Billy and a pig called Honkers? The boy whose underground home was washed away, like hundreds of others along the riverbanks? Did he and his family leave for the goldfields? Or did they stay, and perhaps find a place to live in the town?

What happened to them all?

"Vanilla," Jackson said finally to his mother. "Thanks."

He then sat down outside the ice cream shop, opened his phone again and renamed the photo *Creek Street*.